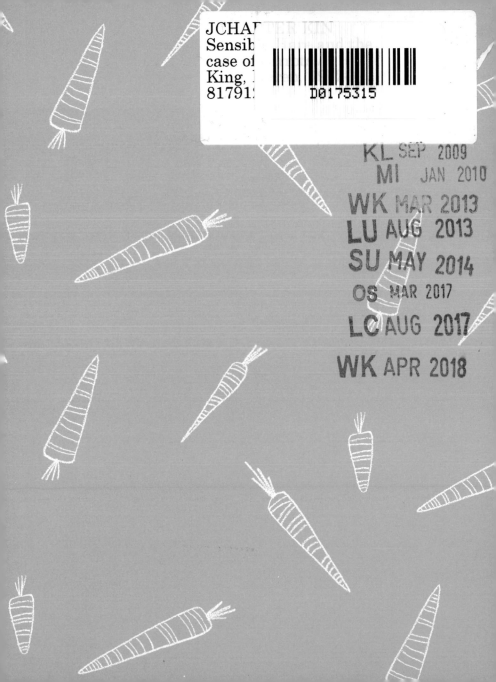

SENSIBLE HARE

AND THE
CASE OF
CARROTS

Daren King

SENSIBLE HARE

AND THE
CASE OF
CARROTS

Illustrated by
David Roberts

ff

faber and faber

For Rebecca Whowell

First published in 2007
by Faber and Faber Limited
3 Queen Square London WC1N 3AU

Typeset by Faber & Faber Ltd
Printed in England by Mackays of Chatham Plc, Chatham, Kent

A CIP record for this book
is available from the British Library

ISBN 978–0–571–23175–1
ISBN 0–571–23175–6

2 4 6 8 10 9 7 5 3 1

CONTENTS

THE HARE

Sensible Hare was not a sensible hare. But he was a hare, and he had the ears to prove it.

Peer through the glass door of Sensible's office. You can see Sensible with his head buried in the latest issue of *Tail*, his favourite magazine.

Tap the glass with your knuckles. Nothing happens. Just because ears are big does not mean they are listening.

To grab Sensible's attention, you have to

press the buzzer.

BZZZZ!

Through the glass, between the stencilled letters SENSIBLE HARE, HARE DETECTIVE, you watch Sensible hop across the room and check his ears in the mirror.

Your ears are big too. Put them to the glass. What do you hear?

Hop!

Hop!

Hop!

That's the sound of Sensible's big furry feet as he hops across the carpet to the door.

THE RABBIT

Do you know the difference between a hare
and a rabbit?

Hares are bigger than rabbits. Hares have
biscuit-coloured fur, and ears that fold in the
middle.

Rabbit ears are small and silky. On a
Tuesday afternoon in late autumn, Sensible
opened the door to the silkiest ears he had
ever seen.

The ears were so silky, the fur so white, the

eyes so ruby-red, Sensible lost
his cool and slammed the door
in the rabbit's face.

Sensible's office used to be an
old hat shop, Horrendous Hats
For All Occasions, where
posh ladies bought hats
for the races. The shop's
old name could still be read
above the shop window in bold
brass letters.

When the posh ladies left, they took the
hats with them. All that remained were the
ghost hats that floated above Sensible's head,
and the ornate mirror where Sensible checked
his ears.

'Wow! She's really, I mean, she's really

something!' Sensible muttered, smoothing his fur. 'I, on the other carrot, look awful.'

Sensible did look awful. He looked like he had been dragged through a hedge by his tail.

An angry hedge.

A hedge with a grudge.

The hedge had roughed him up, stuffed straw in his ears and kicked him into a ditch.

'A rabbit like her,' he said to himself, 'could never like a hare like me.'

Sensible spread a tablecloth over the suitcase he used as a desk, topped it off with a vase of carrots, twitched his tail and opened the door.

'Is this the office of Sensible Hare, Hare Detective?' the rabbit asked. 'I have a case for him.'

'Come in,' Sensible said, hopping to one side. 'Sensible will be with you in one moment.'

The rabbit skipped into the office and closed the door. She looked him up and down carefully. 'Are you sure you're not Sensible Hare?'

'I'm too daft to be Sensible,' said Sensible. 'Sensible has tidy ears, and his feet are as fast as kung fu. Mine are just floppy.' He held up his big furry feet. One at a time, so that he didn't fall over.

'He sounds like just the hare I've been looking for,' the rabbit said. 'Will you fetch him?'

Sensible opened the door, hopped out into the street, and closed the door behind him.

When he returned a minute later, his ears
were tidy and his feet were as fast as kung fu.

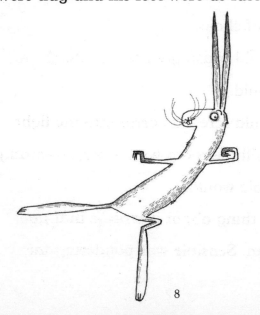

CARROTS

Carrots were Sensible Hare's snack of choice. In fact, carrots were Sensible Hare's everything of choice.

If you could brush your teeth with them, Sensible would.

If you could screw a carrot into the light fitting and fill the room with a carroty-orange glow, Sensible would.

The best thing about carrots is that you can eat them. Sensible was pondering this

fact when the rabbit began her tale.

'My name is Mazy,' the rabbit said, 'and I'm a rabbit.'

Sensible wrote this down in his detective notebook. 'Last name?'

'Rabbit,' said the rabbit.

'Mazy Rabbit?'

Mazy Rabbit nodded her rabbit head. 'I

fled the countryside when the farmer ploughed the field. I left in a hurry, and all I could carry was my huge brown suitcase.'

'Huge?'

Mazy looked down at the tablecloth that covered Sensible's suitcase desk. 'About the size of this table.'

'And what was inside the suitcase?'

'Carrots.'

'Anything else?'

Mazy twitched her nose. 'More carrots.'

'And what happened to this huge brown suitcase?' Sensible asked, lifting his feet onto the desk.

'Stolen,' the rabbit said. 'I left the suitcase on the luggage rack and hopped into my seat. When the train arrived at City Station, the suitcase was gone.'

'And the carrots?'

Mazy looked confused. 'The carrots were inside the suitcase.'

'And where was the inside of the suitcase?'

'The inside of the suitcase was inside the suitcase, with the carrots.'

Sensible frowned a biscuit-coloured frown.

'Do you think you will be able to find it?'

'It could be anywhere by now, Mazy.'

The rabbit's eyes filled with tears. The tears smelt of parsley. 'They told me your ears were tidy. They told me your feet were as fast as kung fu.'

Sensible looked up at his floppers. 'As furry as kung fu, you mean.'

'So you won't help me?'

'Come back one week today,' Sensible said. 'The suitcase of carrots will be here, in this office.'

Mazy Rabbit kissed Sensible on the ear and hopped off.

MR RATCHET

The third time Sensible opened the door that autumn afternoon, he stood ears to knees with Mr Ratchet, the landlord.

Sensible Hare was behind with the rent. He had paid the previous month by selling the furniture. All that remained were the filing cabinet and the huge brown suitcase that Sensible used as a desk.

'Mr, I mean, what I mean is,' Sensible said, not very sensibly.

'You daft hare,' said Mr Ratchet. 'Hop aside and let me in.'

Sensible Hare hopped away from the door.

Mr Ratchet was a big man, and not in a nice way. He was so big, he carried three smaller Mr Ratchets in his overall pocket. These Mr Ratchets came in handy when Mr Ratchet had jobs to do, as you will see.

'Did you, um, pop round to say hello?'

'I would rather eat an earthquake than say hello to you,' Mr Ratchet said, and he meant it.

Sensible hid behind the filing cabinet.

'Tidy this place up. And get these ghosts out of here,' Mr Ratchet said, brushing spooky hats from his hair. 'I told you, no pets.'

Sensible tried to climb out of the window, but Mr Ratchet had him by the tail.

'You are behind with the rent,' Mr Ratchet said. 'If you do not pay the rent today, I will eat your head.'

'My head?'

Mr Ratchet nodded.

'Not the ears,' Sensible said. 'Just the head.'

'The ears and the head.'

Sensible thought about this. 'Ears first?'

'Ears first.'

It is not easy to make a hare angry. The easiest way to make a hare angry is to tug its ears. Threaten to eat them and the hare will be hopping mad.

'Right,' Sensible said, looking down at his floppers. 'Kung-fu feet, do your fastest!'

Sensible was about to leap into the air
when he found himself pinned to the floor by
the three smaller Mr Ratchets, who had
climbed out of Mr Ratchet's overall pocket.

OTTOMAN OTTER

The three smaller Mr Ratchets were about to shut Sensible's ears in the bottom drawer of the filing cabinet when something exciting happened.

In one corner of Sensible's office was a little wooden door. Behind the door was a cupboard, and in that cupboard lived an otter named Ottoman.

Ottoman shared the cupboard with a spider web, and a thimble which he had

decorated with a price ticket and two dabs of
paint. He had named the thimble Thimble,
after his grandma, Thimble Otter, who had
been named after a thimble.

When Ottoman heard the commotion, he
put on his spectacles, hid Thimble behind the
spider web and opened the cupboard door.

Ottoman walked up to Mr Ratchet, walked
up the front of Mr Ratchet's overalls and up
onto the top of Mr Ratchet's head.

The atmosphere in the room was electric.

The three smaller Mr Ratchets let go of
Sensible and looked up at the unexpected
otter.

Sensible sat up and rubbed his eyes with
his ears.

Mr Ratchet had never had an otter stand
on his head before, and did not know what to
do.

Ottoman walked down the front of Mr
Ratchet's head and stood on Mr Ratchet's
nose. 'You are otterly, otterly horrid,'
Ottoman said. 'Get out of Sensible's office,
and take your smaller Mr Ratchets with you.'

Mr Ratchet put the smaller Mr Ratchets
into his overall pocket, apologised to Sensible
Hare, and walked out into the street.

HARE SHAMPOO

'Why are you washing your ears?' Ottoman asked, but Sensible did not hear. He had his ears in a bucket of water.

Sensible pulled his sopping ears from the bucket, grabbed a bottle of Hare Shampoo, and lathered up.

'Why are you washing your ears?' Ottoman asked again. 'You have to find Mazy Rabbit's suitcase.'

'I don't know where it is, Ottoman.'

'That is why you have to find it,' Ottoman said, balancing on the rim of the bucket. 'You have to investigate. You have to look for clues.'

Sensible thought. 'The suitcase was stolen at the station. I could look for clues there.'

'Otterly spot on,' said Ottoman.

Sensible hopped over the bucket and out into the street.

'Don't forget to rinse your ears,' Ottoman

said, but too late. The soapy ears were halfway to City Station.

To reach the station, Sensible had to hop down Market Ruse, a street famous for its criminal hideouts.

A villain named Patrick Quilt was leaning against a lamp-post, picking his fingernails with the blade of a dagger. The moment he saw the hare, he slipped into the nearest phone box and called the VRN, Villain's Radio Network, a radio show listened to only by criminals.

The word was out. Sensible Hare was hopping around town, leaving a trail of bubbles wherever he went.

Within minutes, Sensible was being followed by every villain in the city.

There were villains in rubbish bins,

villains behind villains,

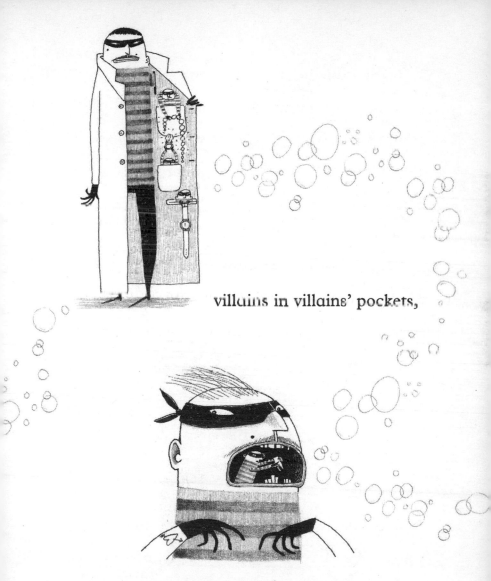

villains in villains' pockets,

villains in villains' mouths.

As Sensible hopped up to the station entrance, hop hop hop, a pair of shoes stepped into his path. These were the shoes of Jack Gin, a villain who had spent five years in prison after Sensible caught him stealing pearls.

Today was Jack Gin's first day of freedom. He had intended to spend the day plotting to murder the Queen, but when he heard the announcement on VRN, he knew he had to pay the hare a visit.

Jack Gin grinned. 'I done time for you.'

'Oh,' said Sensible. 'What I mean is, um, I mean, oh.'

Jack Gin reached out his villainous hands and grabbed Sensible Hare by the nose.

Hares have an inbuilt security system.

Grab the nose and the ears spring forward, whacking you in the face.

This is precisely what happened to Jack Gin. The shampoo stung his eyes and made him cry out. When the villain opened his eyes, the world looked sparkly and clean. But there was no Sensible Hare.

LOST PROPERTY

At City Station, Sensible hopped up to the
ticket inspector, hop hop hop, and asked him
if he had seen any clues.

'Booze?' yelled the ticket inspector. Years of
working on the noisy train platform had
made him deaf. 'What sort of booze?'

'Clues. To help me find a suitcase of
carrots.'

'Booze won't help you find a suitcase of
parrots. Try the Lost Property office.'

Sensible hopped up and down the station platform, hop hop hop, until he found a door with the words LOST PROPERTY stencilled on the glass. He turned the handle and hopped in through the door.

'I'm looking for clues,' Sensible said, not very sensibly.

'What do these clues look like?' asked the woman at the counter.

'I won't know until I find them. I'm a detective, on the trail of a suitcase of carrots.'

The woman rummaged through a large wooden trunk. 'We have a suitcase of parrots. Booze, too. Keys, hankies, wallets. But no carrots.'

Sensible twitched his tail.

The City Station security guard was also

in the Lost Property office, trying on a pair of underpants. 'I saw a suitcase of carrots yesterday afternoon,' he said, putting the underpants on his head. Years of working in security had made him insane. 'I didn't look inside the suitcase, but it smelt of carrots and had carrot leaves poking out the side. I thought it might be

a vegetable bomb, so I chased the owner down the street.'

'What did the owner look like?'

'He was about this height,' the security guard said, holding his hand level with his knee. 'I chased him down Market Ruse and on to the High Street. He went into that old hat shop, Horrendous Hats For All Occasions.'

'You should have followed him inside,' the woman said, 'and made an arrest.'

The security guard turned white. 'Are you mad? That shop is full of ghost hats!'

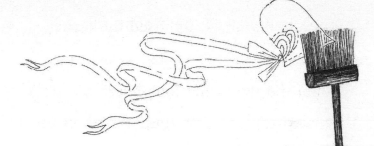

GHOST HATS

Sensible returned to the office to find

Ottoman at the top of a ladder,

brushing the ceiling with a broom.

'What are you doing, Ottoman?'

'Brushing away the ghost hats.'

'Be careful or you'll fall off!'

'No I won't.'

'You will, Ottoman.

You're falling already.'

Sensible was right.

Ottoman had pushed the broom into a particularly poky corner and toppled off the ladder.

'Be careful when you land, Otto. You could hurt yourself.'

'Ouch! Oh, I haven't landed yet. Here I go.' And Ottoman landed on the floor, on his head.

Sensible frowned.

'I wonder,' Ottoman wondered, 'why I fell so slowly.'

'The broom is full of ghost hats.'

Sensible was right. The hats had caught in the bristles, forming a spectral headwear parachute.

Ottoman put the broom into the broom cupboard and closed the door. 'What

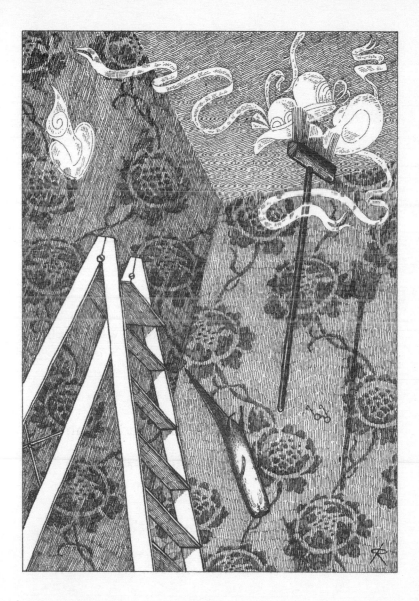

happened at the station? Did you find any clues?'

'The security guard saw a man with a suitcase of carrots yesterday afternoon.'

'Um. What did this man look like?'

'He was about this height,' said Sensible, holding his hand level with the top of Ottoman's head.

Ottoman said nothing.

'The security guard reckons he came in here. Surely we would have seen him.' Sensible sat on the suitcase desk and thought. 'Hmm. You were here yesterday afternoon, Otto. Did you see him?'

Ottoman shook his head.

'This desk is as clean as a peeled carrot,' said Sensible.

'I took it to the cleaners. I have to go to my cupboard now, Sensible. Goodnight.' Ottoman disappeared through the little wooden door, slamming it shut with his tail.

Sensible grabbed a carrot from behind his ear and took a bite.

Carrots are very good for you. Not only do they help you see in the dark, but they also contain a problem-solving vitamin, Carotene-A. Whenever Sensible was stuck with a problem, he would eat a carrot, and in the twitch of a tail the problem would be solved.

The cleaners was on the other side of the city. What if Ottoman had been to the cleaners yesterday morning? He would have arrived at City Station during the afternoon, dragging the huge brown suitcase behind him.

The security guard hadn't seen Mazy's suitcase. He had seen Sensible's suitcase, the huge brown suitcase he used as a desk!

Sensible knocked on the cupboard door with his paw. 'Ottoman? I want a word.'

THE HOPS

Sensible's favourite pub was called The Hops, and it was very popular with hares and rabbits.

There was one rabbit in The Hops today who made Sensible's eyes pop out.

That rabbit was Mazy.

When Mazy saw Sensible at the bar, ordering a pint of carrot juice, she smiled and waved at him with her paw.

Sensible did not hop over.

Mazy fluttered her long eyelashes.

Sensible did not hop over.

Mazy Rabbit hopped onto the table, poked
her snow-white bottom in the air, and
twitched her tail.

If there was one thing that could make
Sensible hop across a crowded pub, it was
Mazy's tail. He stirred his drink with a carrot,
hopped off his barstool and landed at Mazy's
table with a furry thud.

'Sensible! I thought you'd be out catching
villains. Any luck with my suitcase?'

Sensible frowned a biscuit-coloured frown.
'The thing is, Mazy, I mean, um, no.'

Mazy looked disappointed. 'I thought your
ears were tidy. I thought your feet were as
fast as kung fu.'

Sensible looked up at his foldy ears, then down at his floppy feet. He tried to speak, but his mouth was as dry as a sun-dried carrot.

'I have to go,' Mazy said. She took a sip from her lettuce-leaf cocktail and hopped off.

A TWO-CARROT PROBLEM

Ottoman was pacing up and down, his claws behind his back. 'What we need, Sensible, is a clue.'

'This is a two-carrot problem,' said Sensible. 'And it needs a two-carrot solution.' He took two carrots from a grocery bag and crunched.

'Maybe you should pace up

and down,' said Ottoman.

'Shh! I'm thinking.'

'You know what is good for thinking, Sensible.'

'Carrots?'

'Pacing,' said Ottoman, pacing. 'It helps you ponder.' He paced and pondered and paced, but Sensible just sat and crunched.

Ottoman grabbed the carrots from Sensible's mouth and dropped them onto the carpet.

Sensible was surprised. He had never had carrots grabbed from his mouth before and did not know what to do.

'Carrots,' said Ottoman, with whiskery mystery.

Sensible hopped across the room, hop hop

hop, and looked down at the carrots.

Ottoman gave the carrots a kick. They rolled behind the ornate mirror where Sensible checked his ears.

Sensible just stood there, carrotless.

Ottoman cleared his throat. 'Er-herm!'

'Would you like a throat pastille, Ottoman?'

'Your carrots are behind the mirror.'

'Behind the, um. Hmm.' Sensible hopped behind the mirror and picked up one of the carrots.

Ottoman followed. 'The clue could be right here, behind this very mirror.'

Sensible scratched his left ear with his right ear.

'Ooh,' said Ottoman. 'I nearly brushed my

whiskers against a clue by mistake.'

Sensible nodded, said nothing.

Ottoman grabbed Sensible by the ears, and pulled him down to where a red leather strap poked out from a crack in the wall.

Sensible's eyes widened. 'Otto, step aside! The carrots have done the trick. I have found a clue. And just think, it was right under my nose all along!'

Ottoman sighed an ottery sigh.

'It looks like a leather strap, Otto. The sort you find on a lady's handbag or a gentleman's coat.'

'Or a suitcase,' said Ottoman. 'You know what we have to do, Sensible.'

'Visit the greengrocer?'

'We investigate the clue.' Ottoman gave the

leather strap a tug. It came loose, but not before the wall shifted forward, revealing a secret passage.

'Ottoman, fetch the carrots. We are about to have the adventure of our lives!'

CARROT CANDLES

The passage led deep into the damp earth.
Behind, they could see the opening in the wall
and the ornate mirror where Sensible checked
his ears. Ahead they could see nothing but the
tip of Sensible's nose.

If you ever doubt that carrots help you see
in the dark, try using them as candles. The
orange flames danced on the earthy walls,
and on the roots of trees.

'We should have tied a length of string to

the mirror, Otto, so we can find our way back.'

'You can't get lost in a straight line.'

'I can,' Sensible said, not very sensibly.

After more hops than Sensible could count, they found a wooden trapdoor in the tunnel roof.

Sensible scratched his left ear. 'Hmm.'

'I could stand on your head,' said Ottoman, who was as brave as three Sensibles put together. He walked up Sensible's furry back, up onto the top of Sensible's head, and pushed open the trapdoor with his paws. 'Oh dear.'

'Ottoman?'

'Yes?'

'Why did you say oh dear?'

'Oh dear,' said Ottoman, saying oh dear again. 'Oh dear oh dear oh dear,' he said, adding three more.

'Oh dear oh dear oh dear what?'

'Villains,' Ottoman whispered. 'This tunnel leads directly beneath Market Ruse!'

'What are the villains doing?'

'Playing poker. Wow, that villain has a terrific hand.'

'Tell me, Otto. Kings? Aces?'

'Rings,' said Ottoman. 'Gold rings. I wish I had hands, Sensible. Claws are horrid.'

HARRY BAD

This was the villains' Top Secret Hideout,
deep beneath the cellars of Market Ruse.

The villains were sitting around one of
several barrels of whisky, eating peanuts and
shouting.

'Let's rob a bank!'

'Nah. Let's kill the mayor.'

'How do we do that? Poison?'

'Stab him in the guts.'

One of the villains thumped the barrel with

his fist. This was Uncle Carbuncle, the most famous villain in the city. 'Concentrate on the game. I got five jacks and an ace.'

The other villains were unimpressed.

'You can't have an ace. I got all twelve right here.'

'Never mind that. Who can top a queen of kings?'

'I got a joker!'

Uncle Carbuncle pulled out a gun and shot the joker six times. 'The six of bullets. Beat that!'

One by one, the villains threw in their cards.

'Wait!' said a voice. Out of a shady corner stepped a villain none of the villains had ever seen before. 'I'm Harry Bad, and I'm taking you lot to the cleaners.'

Harry Bad turned to face Sensible and Ottoman, who cowered in the dark by the trapdoor. Both knew what would happen if they were seen. The villains would turn them into hare and otter pâté, with a side helping of carrot relish.

But Harry Bad was not looking at Sensible and Ottoman.

'That,' said Harry Bad, pointing towards a red leather case, 'is a suitcase what I nicked. It is full of green stuff.'

The words were cleverly chosen. To a villain, green stuff is money. In those days, most banknotes were as green as carrot leaves.

Mazy's suitcase of carrots?

'The contents of this suitcase are my stake,' said Harry Bad, pulling up a stool. 'Deal the cards.'

KUNG-FU FEET

Sensible scratched his left ear and thought. He scratched his right ear and thought. When he ran out of ears he scratched Ottoman's ears, but that didn't help because otter ears are tiny.

Suddenly, Sensible knew what he had to do. Mazy Rabbit's suitcase had been stolen. And here, in this room, was the thief.

'Stop scratching my ears,' Ottoman whispered.

'Sorry, Otto. Let's grab the

case and hop it.' Sensible dropped the red leather case through the closed trapdoor, which splintered into tiny pieces, and hopped into the tunnel.

All eyes turned to Ottoman, apart from the eyes of Blind Huey, who was deaf and had not heard the crash.

The villains leapt from their stools.

'Grab him, quick!'

'Otter pie!'

Ottoman's life flashed before him. He had spent most of it in the cupboard with Thimble, so it was not very interesting, but it was his life and he intended to keep it. He leapt into the tunnel, and landed on Sensible's head with an ouch.

Sensible lit a carrot candle. 'Which way?'

The tunnel looked identical in both directions, so he grabbed Ottoman and the red leather case and followed his floppy feet.

'I don't remember these rocks,' said Ottoman. 'We must be going the wrong way.'

The villains were fast runners, but they kept tripping over their swag bags and

picking each other's pockets, which gave
Sensible and Ottoman time to get ahead.

Then, disaster!

The tunnel came to a dead end.

Sensible dropped the case and turned to
face the villains. 'Kung-fu feet, do your
fastest!' One by one, he sent the villains
hurtling into the circular darkness.

Ottoman tapped the tunnel wall with his
claws.

Tap tap.

Tap.

Clang!

Clang clang!

'Metal,' said Ottoman. 'Some sort of
ventilation shaft.'

Sensible lowered the carrot candle. The

panel was held in place with two screws, one at the top and one at the bottom. Ottoman unscrewed the top screw with his claw and the panel sprang open.

'What about the suitcase, Otto? It won't fit through.'

'Bury it.'

Sensible dug a kung-fu hole and buried the red leather case in the earth.

The villains arrived just in time to see Sensible's tail disappear through the ventilation shaft.

'What do we do?' asked Jack Gin.

Uncle Carbuncle bent his knees and peered into the shaft. 'We follow.'

KUNG-FU EARS

When the villains emerged from the
ventilation shaft, they had the surprise of their
lives. The ground beneath them seemed to
shudder and shake.

'Earthquake!'

'Help!'

The last villain to arrive was Deaf Louie, who was as blind as Blind Huey was deaf.

'This ain't no earthquake,' said Deaf Louie. Being blind had sharpened his other senses. 'This is the movement of a high-speed locomotive.'

The villains looked around. They were in a crowded passenger train. The windows were a blur of greenery and blurry blue.

'Where did they go?'

Blind Huey pointed towards the front of the train, where a pair of foldy ears poked from the top of a businessman's head. 'There!'

The villains grabbed their swag bags and chased the hare and the otter up the carriage.

Passengers turned and stared. They were

not pleased, particularly when the villains stole their jewellery.

In the driver's compartment, the train driver was fast asleep. Even the arrival of a hare, an otter, several villains and eight angry passengers with empty pockets failed to wake him.

Ottoman leapt out through the driver's window and scrambled up onto the train roof.

Sensible had no choice but to follow.

The view from the train roof was incredible. They could see the line of wobbling carriages, and the train track retreating into the distance. Woods, hills and lakes vanished over the horizon.

'We're safe up here,' said Sensible, the wind whistling through his ears, 'as long as we keep our balance.'

'Not if the villains come after us.'

'They won't come up here, Otto. They're not that stupid.'

But the villains were that stupid.

A hand appeared, decorated with flashing diamond rings. The hand of Uncle Carbuncle.

Sensible hopped it.

The frightening thing about hopping along the roof of a moving train is that you hop fifty times faster than you would on the ground. Sensible hopped so high, he hopped right off the end of the train.

At times like these, Sensible's ears were more kung fu than his feet. The left ear grabbed hold of the back of the train and swung the hare through an open window, where he landed safely in a fat man's lap.

But where was Ottoman?

The brave otter was still up on the train roof!

When Uncle Carbuncle saw Ottoman staring at him with otter hatred, he stopped dead. The other villains peered over his villainous shoulders, eyes fixed on the unexpected otter.

The atmosphere on the train roof was electric.

Uncle Carbuncle had never had an otter stare at him before, and did not know what to do.

Ottoman walked up to Uncle Carbuncle, walked up the front of the stripy sweater and up onto the top of Uncle Carbuncle's head.

HAROLD GOOD

He walked down the villain's forehead and stepped onto the big, bulbous nose. 'You are otterly, otterly horrid,' Ottoman said. 'Leave us alone. Or we will call the police.'

When Ottoman returned to the secret passage, the villains did not follow. Sensible dug the red leather case out of the kung-fu hole and carried it back to the office, where Ottoman polished the leather until it shone.

'When Mazy sees this suitcase,' said

Sensible, 'she will fall in love with me, and kiss me on the nose.'

Ottoman looked shifty.

'If you're worried about the leather strap, Otto, we can sew it back on.'

BZZZZ!

Sensible hopped across the room to check his ears in the mirror. He covered the suitcase desk with the tablecloth, placed the red leather case on top, and opened the door.

'Am I in the office of Sensible Hare, Hare Detective?'

This was not Mazy Rabbit.

Sensible had seen this man before, but he could not put his carrot on it.

Perhaps it was the false beard? Or the plastic nose and the big rubber ears? Perhaps it was the dark glasses, or the glass eyes, stuck to each lens with sticky tape?

If Sensible had known better, if he had been sensible, he would have suspected this man of wearing a disguise.

'My name is Harold Good,' the man said, 'and I have a case for you. The case of a stolen case.'

Sensible looked at Ottoman.

Ottoman looked at Sensible.

Sensible hopped to the mirror and looked at himself.

'Ah!' said Harold Good when he saw the red leather case. 'That was quick. What do I owe you?' He undid the latch and opened the lid.

The red leather case did not contain carrots as they had thought. It was packed with crisp green banknotes.

Harold handed Sensible a bundle of notes, thanked him, tucked the red leather case under his arm and left the office.

ARREST

Sensible was about to remove the tablecloth from the suitcase desk when the buzzer buzzed again.

BZZZZ!

Sensible didn't bother to check his ears this time. He let them hang in front of his face, like tatty cardboard.

Mazy stood on the doorstep, twitching her nose. 'I hear you found my suitcase! I'm very impressed.'

Sensible shook his head, said nothing.

Ottoman grabbed Sensible's tail and pulled him away from the door with three backwards hops, poh poh poh.

'You have found my suitcase, haven't you, Sensible?'

'If you could wait a few more days,' Ottoman said, 'Sensible will have the case solved. He has clues poking out of his ears.'

Mazy's ruby-red eyes twinkled with hope.

But Sensible shook his head. 'Sorry, Mazy. I am not a sensible hare at all. I'm a daft hare, with feet as floppy as carrot leaves.'

Mazy reached out a soft white paw to touch him.

Suddenly, the door burst open and the room was full of police officers, holding guns

and cups of tea.

'Sensible Hare,' said the Police Sergeant, 'you are under arrest for handling stolen luggage.'

The Police Sergeant held out a photograph of the old hat shop. Through the glass door, between the stencilled letters SENSIBLE HARE, HARE DETECTIVE, stood the daft hare, the red leather case in his paws.

'That case has been reported stolen,' the Sergeant explained. 'It was nabbed by a villain named Harry Bad. The case has now been returned to its rightful owner, Harold Good.'

'But I handed it to Harold Good myself,' Sensible said.

'Ah,' said the Police Sergeant. 'So you

admit it.'

'This is otterly outrageous,' said Ottoman.

'This,' said the Sergeant, 'is justice.'

Two uniformed officers grabbed Sensible by the ears and fastened his wrists with pawcuffs. The poor hare was dragged outside and bundled into the back of a police van.

Through the back window, Sensible could see Ottoman and Mazy Rabbit on the kerb. A parsley tear twinkled in Mazy's eye.

SAD-SACK HARE

That night, Sensible lay alone in a prison cell at the back of the police station. Tomorrow, the judge would decide his fate. For now, he could only lie on his sack and think of Mazy.

Through the tiny window, high above Sensible's ears, the moon hung in the sky, round as carrot pie.

Sensible tried to stay awake, but his left ear flopped in front of his left eye. He moved it aside with his paw, but then the right ear flopped in front of his right eye, so he pushed that aside too. When both ears flopped, the world went black and Sensible was asleep.

In his dream, he hopped up the cell wall and pushed his paw through the bars, but the carrot-pie moon was out of reach.

Suddenly, he was awoken by a scraping sound.

Scrape!

Scrape scrape!

Scrape scrape scrape!

Daylight streamed through the window. Sensible's kung-fu eyes darted about the cell, but everything looked normal.

Then, a brick fell from the wall.

Sensible caught the brick on his head.

'Ouch,' he thought. 'Hmm.'

Peering through the hole, he could see a claw. And then he heard a friendly voice.

'Sensible? Have I got the right cell?'

Ottoman!

Another brick was pushed through, then three more. Sensible caught each brick with his kung-fu feet and lowered them to the concrete floor.

Ottoman pushed the last two bricks out together. Sensible caught them both, one on each foot, but fell flat on his tail. The bricks flew over his ears and hit the far wall with a thud.

From the other side of the cell door, Sensible's ears heard the sound of footsteps, followed by voices and the rattle of keys.

The police entered the cell just in time to see Sensible's tail disappear through the hole.

UNMASKED

Sensible and Ottoman ran down the damp tunnel.

With no carrot candle to light the way, Sensible could only follow the scratch and scrape of Ottoman's claws.

The tunnel was so dark the police officers kept spilling their tea. There were a dozen of them, blowing their whistles and shouting.

'Halt! Arrest! Stop!'

On and on they ran, claws, paws and

boots, until without warning the tunnel opened out into a large underground room.

The villains' Top Secret Hideout, deep beneath the cellars of Market Ruse!

Any other day, the villains would have been ready, but they had been up all night drinking whisky to celebrate Sensible's arrest.

Jack Gin had a headache bigger than his head. Deaf Louie and Blind Huey both felt seasick. Patrick Quilt was fast asleep, upside-down, his head in a whisky barrel.

Uncle Carbuncle reached into his pocket for his gun, but pulled out an empty beer bottle.

The police officers did not know who to arrest first, so they decided to arrest everyone at once.

A moment later, the room was a riot of playing cards, teacups and whisky. Several policemen wrestled an empty raincoat to the floor. Another handcuffed himself to a table leg. Whistles were blown, fists were thrown, shots were fired and kung-fu feet kicked.

When the dust settled, the villains found themselves handcuffed together, along

with three police officers and one of Sensible's ears.

'Could you, um, release my ear?' Sensible said, not very sensibly.

'Let him go,' Ottoman demanded. 'He's a hare detective, not a villain.'

'This hare is an escaped criminal,' said the Police Sergeant. 'I arrested him myself just yesterday, for handling a stolen case.'

'What if that case was never actually stolen? What if Harold Good pretended his case was stolen, so that Sensible would be locked up?'

The Police Sergeant was baffled.

Sensible was baffled too. His ears were baffled, his tail was bewildered, and his furry feet were perplexed.

'If only Harold Good was here,' said Ottoman, almost to himself.

The Police Sergeant took a sip from his tea.

'Yes,' said Ottoman cleverly. 'If only Harold Good was in this room right now. Inside this whisky barrel, tied up.' He pushed the barrel onto its side, and out tumbled Harold Good, bound with rope.

'Untie him!' said the Police Sergeant. 'Harold Good is a respectable citizen.'

Ottoman leant Harold Good against the wall and removed the glass eyes, stuck to Harold's glasses with sticky tape.

'I don't understand,' the Police Sergeant said.

Ottoman removed Harold's dark glasses

and dropped them into a barrel of whisky. Splosh!

'I'm still no wiser,' the Police Sergeant said.

Ottoman removed Harold Good's big rubber ears.

'Perhaps I should retire,' the Police Sergeant said.

Ottoman plucked the plastic nose from Harold's face and tossed it over his shoulder.

It was only when Ottoman removed Harold Good's false beard that the Sergeant understood. 'Harry Bad!'

'That's right,' said Ottoman. 'Harry Bad and Harold Good are the same person. The red leather case was not stolen at all.'

'Sensible Hare,' said the Police Sergeant, eating his words, 'you and your pet otter are free to go. As for you villains, you are all under arrest.'

GHOST CARROTS

Sensible Hare arrived at work the next day to find the office swarming with ghost carrots.

Sensible thought he had died and gone to hare heaven.

'Otto?'

'Up here.'

Sensible looked up to see the otter halfway up a ladder with a large metal contraption.

'What have you got there?'

'This?' Ottoman said innocently. 'A film

projector, projecting images of spooky carrots. I wonder how that got there!'

'No time for practical jokes, Otto. Mazy Rabbit will be here at any moment. That must be her now.'

BZZZZ!

Otto switched off the projector and climbed down.

Sensible hopped across the room to check his ears in the mirror. He covered the suitcase desk with the tablecloth and opened the door.

'Pay up, or I pull your ears off!'

This was not Mazy Rabbit.

This was Mr Ratchet, the landlord.

'I don't have the um, I mean, what I mean is,' Sensible said, not very sensibly.

'You daft hare,' Mr Ratchet said, and

reached into his overall pocket.

'Keep your three smaller Mr Ratchets to yourself,' said Ottoman. He took a bundle of bunknotes from his cupboard and handed them to the landlord.

'Where did you get the money?' asked Sensible when Mr Ratchet had gone.

'From Harold Good. Or should I say Harry Bad? Remember the money he gave us when we handed him the red leather case?'

BZZZZ!

'It's her,' Ottoman said. 'Check your ears and let her in.'

Sensible hopped up to the mirror, and hid behind it.

'Why are you hiding?'

'I can't let her in, Otto. We haven't solved

the case.'

'Never mind that. Open the door and let her in.'

Sensible hopped out from behind the mirror and hopped across the room to the door.

'Ears,' said Ottoman.

Sensible gave his ears a quick tidy and opened the door.

Mazy's ruby-red eyes sparkled.

The detective hopped up and down with nervous excitement.

'Don't just hop there. Let her in!'

Mazy twitched her snow-white tail and hopped into the office. 'Is it here? Have you found it?'

Sensible shook his head.

Ottoman extended a claw and pointed at

the suitcase desk.

'Hmm,' Sensible said, not very sensibly.

'Look more closely.'

Sensible looked more closely. There, on top of the tablecloth, was Thimble.

'Why is there a thimble on my tablecloth?'

'Don't you recognise him? That's Thimble, who lives behind the spider web in my cupboard.'

'So it is!'

'I think he wants to tell you something.'

Sensible scratched his right knee with his left ear. 'Does he?'

'He wants you to look under the tablecloth.'

Sensible pulled back the tablecloth to reveal the suitcase desk. Thimble fell onto the

floor and rolled under the filing cabinet. His work here was done.

When Mazy saw the suitcase desk, her eyes shone. 'My suitcase!'

Sensible could not have been more confused if you showed him a blue carrot.

Mazy flipped the latch and opened the suitcase. She kissed Sensible on the nose and ears. 'You found it!'

'It must have been here from the start,' Sensible said, not very sensibly.

'What he means,' said Ottoman, 'is that he tracked it down using his radar ears, with kung-fu feet backup.'

Mazy was impressed. 'What do I owe you?'

Sensible thought. 'My usual fee is a suitcase of carrots, but—'

'Then I will leave this here,' Mazy said.
'Perhaps I can cook you a carrot-lit dinner to
thank you?'

Sensible was so happy he could
barely hop.

After Mazy had left, Sensible asked
Ottoman for an explanation.
'You set this up yourself.
You stole the
suitcase from
Mazy so that
she would ask
me to find it
and she would
like me.'

Ottoman smiled
a whiskery smile. 'It

was the day I went to visit my uncle, Uncle Empire. When I saw Mazy on the train, I knew she was the rabbit for you.'

'You were right,' said Sensible.

And he blushed a bright carroty orange.

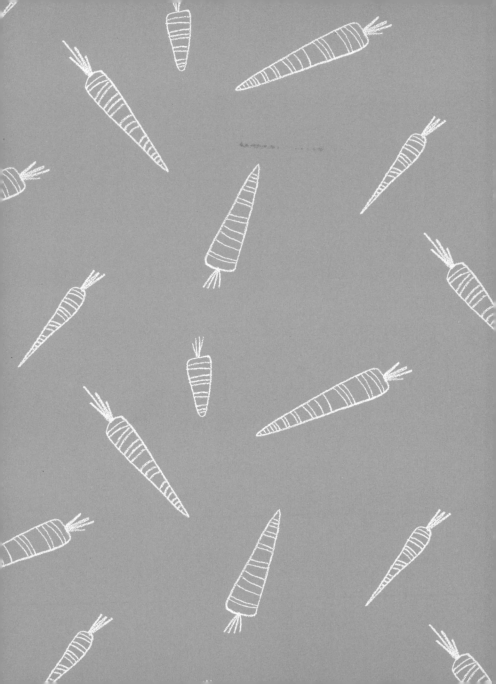